God Needed a Puppy

BY
John Gray

ILLUSTRATED BY
Shanna Brickell

2018 First Printing
God Needed a Puppy

Text copyright © 2018 by John Gray
Illustrations copyright © 2018 by Shanna Obelenus

ISBN 978-1-64060-148-2

The Paraclete Press name and logo (dove on cross) are trademarks of
Paraclete Press, Inc.

Library of Congress Cataloging-in-Publication Data
Names: Gray, John Joseph, 1962- author. | Brickell, Shanna, illustrator
Title: God needed a puppy / John Gray ; illustrated by Shanna Brickell.
Description: Brewster, Massachusetts : Paraclete Press, [2018] | Summary:
   «Edgar the owl and Freddy the fox explain why some pets die young and
   leave their owners very sad. God needed their puppy in heaven for some
   one very special and he will send a new pet to fill its place»—Provided by
   publisher.
Identifiers: LCCN 2018020429 | ISBN 9781640601482 (hardback)
Subjects: | CYAC: Death—Fiction. | Grief—Fiction. | Dogs—Fiction. |
   Pets—Fiction. | Christian life—Fiction. | BISAC: RELIGION / Christian
   Life / Death, Grief, Bereavement. | PETS / Dogs / General. | JUVENILE
   FICTION / Religious / Christian / Animals. | JUVENILE FICTION / Religious /
   Christian / Emotions & Feelings.
Classification: LCC PZ7.1.G733 Go 2018 | DDC [E]—dc23
LC record available at https://lccn.loc.gov/2018020429
10 9 8 7 6 5 4 3 2 1

Published by Paraclete Press
Brewster, Massachusetts
www.paracletepress.com

Printed in the United States of America

To Courtney for believing in me.

To Samuel for inspiring me.

To anyone who has loved and lost a furry best friend.

A moment in our arms, forever in our hearts.

Deep in the forest Edgar the Owl took his nap in the soft needles beneath a big pine tree next to a stream. He'd just fallen asleep when stomping through the woods came a young red fox named Freddy.

"It's not fair, it's not fair," he said.

Edgar awoke and could see the fox was upset, so he whispered, "What's not fair?"

Freddy told him that the little boy who lived in the blue house was in his backyard crying because his dog died.

"He loved that dog," Freddy told Edgar. "I used to watch them play together. Why would God take him away?"

The wise old owl thought for a moment, then said, "Maybe God needed a puppy."

Freddy didn't understand, so Edgar sat next to him on a tree stump and told him a story.

"You know, Freddy, the world would be a pretty boring place if there weren't animals for people to play with."

"Animals like us?" asked the fox.

"That's right, Freddy. Foxes, owls, bunnies, birds, chipmunks, turtles, raccoons, deer, lizards."

"Lizards?" Freddy asked in a silly voice.

"Yes, even lizards." Edgar chuckled.

"But the most special animals God ever made were pets. The cats, dogs, hamsters, even fishes that he sends down to play with little boys and girls."

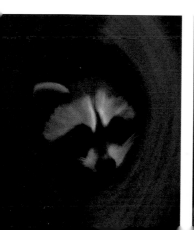  

"Sometimes they live a long time, and sometimes they are only here for a short visit," Edgar said.

"But why can't they stay forever?" asked the fox.

"Different reasons," the owl responded. "Sometimes they have to leave to make room for another pet that is waiting to come down and be with a child, and sometimes they're needed in heaven."

"By God?" Freddy wondered. "Well, sort of, Freddy," Edgar said.

"You see, sometimes there's a child in heaven who needs a puppy or a kitten to play with, so God asks one of the most special ones on earth to please come up and play with them."

The fox scratched his chin. "Is that what happened with that little boy's dog?"

The owl nodded, "I'm sure it is."

He then told Freddy, "Not so long ago there was a little girl named Piper who lived in the yellow house by the lake. I used to watch her from my favorite rock. Piper was in a wheelchair and she was very sick, so she couldn't have a puppy."

"Because she couldn't run and play?" asked the fox.

"That's right, Freddy. But she wanted a puppy really bad," said the owl.

"When she died and went to heaven she wasn't sick or in a wheelchair anymore, so she could play like the other kids. God asked her what she wanted more than anything else. And can you guess what she wanted, Freddy?"

The fox answered quickly, "A puppy?"

"That's right. So, God needed a puppy. But not just any puppy."

The fox yelled, "A SPECIAL PUPPY."

"Right again," the owl said with a smile.

"Now there was a boy named Oliver who had a special puppy named Samuel. He had a black face with light brown eyes and big fluffy ears. He would jump in leaves and chase sticks and play, play, play. Samuel and Oliver loved each other, but one night something happened."

"What?" asked the fox.

"Samuel went to sleep, and God talked to him. He said, I know you're having fun down here with Oliver, but I need a really special puppy in heaven. Can you come with me? I promise you'll see Oliver again someday. Samuel didn't really want to go, but he knew Piper needed him in heaven, so he went."

"But wasn't Oliver sad?" asked Freddy.

"Yes he was, just like that little boy in the blue house. But here's the part you need to understand, Freddy."

The owl put his wing around the fox, giving him a hug. "When we say goodbye to a pet it's not goodbye forever. And sometimes when we are less sad another pet that needs a friend comes down from heaven to be with us."

"And did he? Did God send another dog down to be with Oliver?" asked the fox.

"Yes, he did, Freddy," said the owl. "There was another puppy in heaven named Sebastian who needed a little boy to play with. So, when Samuel came up to heaven to be with Piper, Sebastian went down to be with . . . "

"OLIVER," shouted the fox with joy.

Suddenly Freddy started running toward the path.

"Thanks, Edgar," he said.

"Where are you going?" asked the owl.

"To talk to that little boy in the blue house," said the fox.

"And what are you going to tell him?" shouted the owl.

The fox smiled, "That he shouldn't be sad, because his puppy is in heaven playing, and he'll see him again someday."

"Anything else?" the owl asked.

"Yeah, I'll tell him for now I'll be his friend. The best friend I can be."

As the fox disappeared from sight Edgar looked up at the tall trees and said, "So God needed a puppy and sent a fox to take his place."

Just then all the birds in the forest, like angels above, began to sing, and somewhere in heaven a puppy named Samuel wagged his tail, knowing his friend Oliver, just like you, is going to be OK.